Goodnight Goodnight
SLEEPYHEAD

Originally published as *Eyes Nose Fingers Toes*

by Ruth Krauss

Illustrated by Jane Dyer

HarperCollins Publishers

Goodnight Goodnight Sleepyhead

Text copyright © 1964 by Ruth Krauss

Illustrations copyright © 2004 by Jane Dyer

Text originally published as *Eyes Nose Fingers Toes*, written by Ruth Krauss

Manufactured in China by South China Printing Company Ltd.   All rights reserved.

www.harperchildrens.com

Library of Congress Cataloging-in-Publication Data

Krauss, Ruth.   Goodnight goodnight sleepyhead / by Ruth Krauss ; illustrated by Jane Dyer.

p.   cm.   Text originally published under title: Eyes nose fingers toes: New York : Harper & Row, 1964.

Summary: In simple rhyming text, a child says goodnight to the things around her.

ISBN 0-06-028894-9 – ISBN 0-06-028895-7 (lib. bdg.)

[1. Bedtime–Fiction. 2. Stories in rhyme.] I. Dyer, Jane, ill.

II. Krauss, Ruth. Eyes nose fingers toes. III. Title.

PZ8.3.K865Go 2004   [E]–dc21   2003050805

Typography by Carla Weise

1 2 3 4 5 6 7 8 9 10

❖

First Edition

For my grandniece, Delaney Ann Reimer

—J.D.

Eyes nose
fingers toes
lips hair . . .

everywhere

Goodnight eyes

Goodnight nose

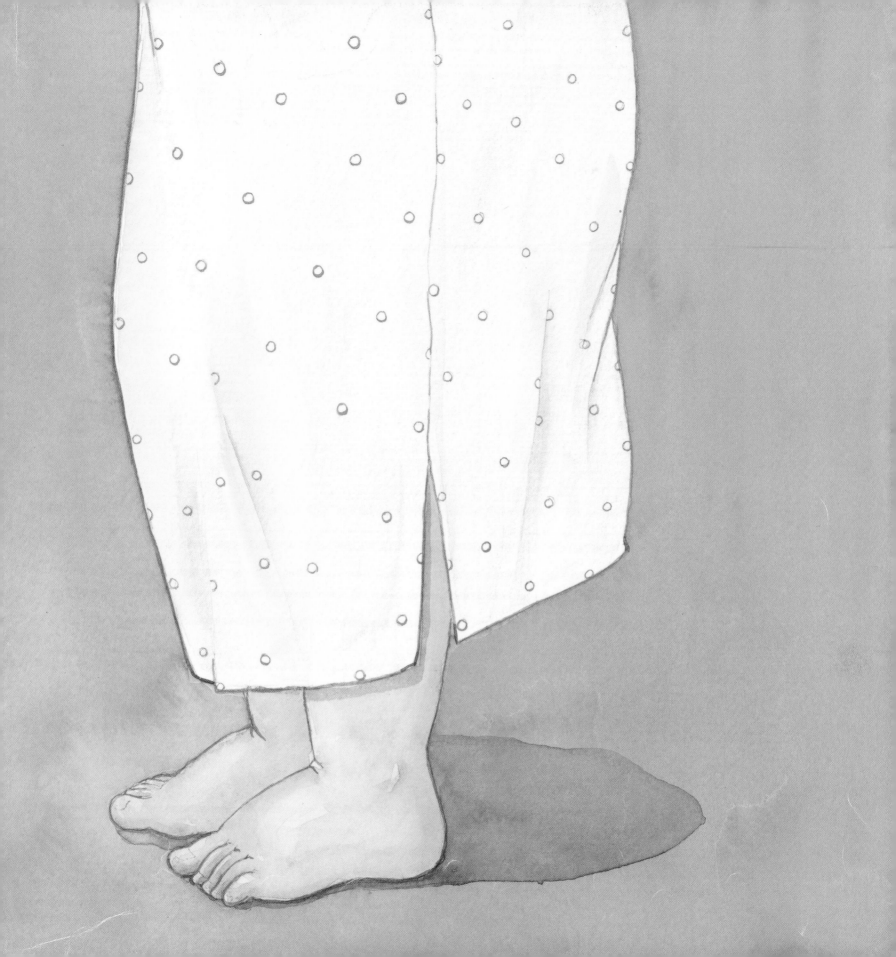

Goodnight lips

Goodnight hair

Goodnight Goodnight
Everywhere

Goodnight windows

Goodnight doors

Goodnight walls

Goodnight floors

Goodnight chairs

Goodnight bed

Goodnight Goodnight
Sleepyhead

eyes nose fingers toes
lips hair everywhere
windows doors walls floors
chairs bed sleepyhead